DANCE TEAM

CHARNAN SIMON

SURVIVING SOUTHSIDE

DANCE TEAM

Charnan Simon

MINNEAPOLIS

Darby Creek
A division of Lerner Publishing Group, Inc.
241 First Avenue North
Minneapolis, MN 55401 U.S.A.

Website address: www.lernerbooks.com

The images in this book are used with the permission of: © Garry Wade/The Image Bank/Getty Images, (main image) front cover; © iStockphoto.com/Jill Fromer, (banner background) front cover and throughout interior; © iStockphoto.com/Naphtalina, (brick wall background) front cover and throughout interior.

Main body text set in Janson Text LT Std 55 Roman 12/17.5.
Typeface provided by Adobe Systems.

Library of Congress Cataloging-in-Publication Data

Simon, Charnan.
    Dance team / by Charnan Simon.
        p.   cm. — (Surviving Southside)
    ISBN 978–1–4677–0313–0 (lib. bdg. : alk. paper)
    [1. Dance teams—Fiction. 2. Dance—Fiction. 3. High
schools—Fiction. 4. Schools—Fiction.] I. Title.
PZ7.S6035Dan 2013
[Fic]—dc23   2012029522

Manufactured in the United States of America
1 – BP – 12/31/12

SURVIVING SOUTHSIDE
YA FIC
SIMO

CHAPTER 1

"**O**kay, cut! Get some water!"

Whew. I had never been so grateful for a water break.

We'd been rehearsing nonstop for nearly an hour, and I was drenched in sweat. Camilla was a great dance team captain, but she didn't go easy on anyone. If she hadn't driven herself even harder than she drove the rest of us, I don't think we'd have been able to stand her.

Maybe I just felt so overworked because I was so new. New to the dance team and new to Southside High. Until the summer before freshman year, my family had lived in the Northside High School district. I always assumed I'd go to Northside with my middle school friends. But my dad switched jobs that spring, and my parents decided it made sense to move closer to his new office. We'd be closer to my grandparents that way too, and my aunt and uncle, which made my mom happy.

I had been shocked. *How can Mom and Dad do this to me?* I wondered. *Who wants to move between middle school and high school?*

I argued as hard as I could, but in the end parents have the final say. And life wasn't all bad after that. For one thing, our new house was a lot nicer than our old one. I liked being close to my Gran and Gramps and cousins. And I was lucky enough to make a new friend my very first day.

Olivia lived three houses down from our new place, in a big, pretty home on the corner.

She and her mom came over with lemonade and a cooler of sandwiches on the day we moved—the hottest day in the middle of the longest heat wave of the summer—and Olivia instantly made me feel welcome.

"I'm so glad you're a girl," she said.

I almost snorted lemonade out my nose. What else would I be?

Olivia laughed. "I mean, I'm glad you're a girl my age, so we can be friends. There's nothing but boys on this block. Little boys, not even high school guys. I haven't had a girlfriend within walking distance since, well, forever."

I could appreciate how Olivia felt. Back home on the north side, my best friend had lived right next door.

Later that afternoon, Olivia helped me unpack my room. That's when she saw all my dance stuff.

"You're a dancer!" she said. "So am I! Oh, this is perfect. I want to try out for Southside's dance team this fall, but I'm too scared to do it by myself. Freshmen hardly ever make the team. Now you can audition with me!"

And that's exactly what happened.

When Olivia found out I'd taken tap and jazz since I was little, she didn't let up. She actually didn't have to work too hard—I'd always wanted to try out for the Northside dance team, but the competition was super tough at my old school. Southside's dance team was newer, and I had a better shot at making it. Plus, Olivia convinced me that joining dance team would be the perfect way to meet other Southside kids.

No one was more surprised than I was when I actually made the team. Olivia made it too. The two of us supported each other through the fall and winter, and then there we were. Halfway into spring term, with regionals less than a month away.

I chugged some water and slid down to the gym floor. Olivia collapsed next to me.

"Camilla's brutal today," Olivia said. "Look—my legs are actually twitching!"

"I know," I agreed. "But we're getting better. Aren't we?"

Even though this was just my first year on dance team, I thought we looked pretty good.

Apparently Camilla didn't agree. "Listen up, everyone!" she called in a sharp voice. I swear she wasn't even breathing hard. "Regionals are in less than a month, and frankly, we're not ready. Northside's won the last three years, and I'm damned if they're going to walk away with that trophy again this time. This is *our* year!"

Then Camilla got specific. Painfully specific. "Ana, your air splits are sloppy—clean them up. Berit, your switch leaps are getting better, but they're still not good enough to win us that trophy. Cate, you're half a beat off when we go into the second V-formation. Trez, fantastic jazz layout!"

Camilla paused, and I breathed a sigh of relief. Maybe I was off the hook this practice.

But no. Camilla looked straight at me and shook her head. "Izzy, I don't know where you learned to do triple pirouettes, but they're pathetic. I took a chance by bringing you on as a freshman, but I'll tell you one thing right now. I'm not taking you to regionals with those pirouettes!"

My cheeks burned. I'd always had trouble with triple pirouettes, but surely they weren't that bad?

Olivia patted my shoulder as Camilla went on to point out the weaknesses of other team members. "Don't worry," she whispered. "Pirouette turns are hard. We'll practice together. You'll be fine!"

I felt a rush of gratitude. Olivia's the only other freshman on the dance team, and we stick together. She's a much better dancer than I am, but she never holds it over me or makes me feel bad. She's a good friend inside and outside of dance team.

I turned my attention back to what Camilla was saying. "Okay, one last thing. I don't think our regular after-school practices are going to be enough. From now on, I'm adding before-school practices on Mondays and Wednesdays to help you guys shape up. Be here at 6:45 A.M. sharp!"

Groans echoed all around. Camilla ignored them. "See you tomorrow morning!" she said sweetly as she headed to the gym door. "Bye!"

CHAPTER 2

I was glum as we gathered up our backpacks and dance bags. "Camilla hates me," I said as we walked to the bus stop. "She's sorry she ever let me on the team!"

Olivia laughed and poked my side. "Oh, poor Izzy," she teased. "One little bit of criticism and you're a goner. It's never personal with Camilla. She's just the most competitive person on the planet. She wants to win! Now, how about you invite me to your house? We can eat some of your mom's cookies and nail those pirouettes."

My mom does make good cookies. She says it's her one bit of domesticity. Mom illustrates children's books for a living. She spends most of her time at a drawing table in the sunny kitchen alcove. Besides the fact that she doesn't really like housekeeping, time tends to get away from Mom when she's drawing.

That afternoon she was hunched over a pen-and-ink drawing of baby ducklings. "Hey, girls," she said when we came in. "What do you think? Did I get the waddle right?"

Mom always gets the waddle right. I wish I could draw like she does.

"Looks super," Olivia said cheerfully. "Do you have any cookies?"

Olivia's not shy.

Mom's face brightened. "I do!" she said. "I got stuck this morning and had to take a baking break. Oatmeal-butterscotch, extra butterscotch chips, no nuts."

Mom put down her drawing pen and came over to the kitchen table to join us in a snack.

She listened sympathetically when I told her what Camilla said about my pirouettes.

"Maybe Leah could help you practice," she suggested when I paused for breath.

"Who's Leah?" asked Olivia through a mouthful of cookie.

I hesitated. Leah Velasco had been my next-door neighbor at our old house. She was two years older than I was, but we had been friends since we were babies. She also happened to be the captain of the Northside High dance team. Leah was a fantastic dancer, and a big reason I'd taken dance classes all my life. She knew I sort of idolized her. She had encouraged me to follow in her footsteps and join Northside's dance team.

But things had changed in the last year. Leah wasn't as happy as I thought she'd be when I called her to say I made Southside's dance team. It was almost like she was jealous of me for getting on the team on my first try. Or like she was mad at herself for wasting all those years coaching me, just so I could be on a rival squad.

Olivia sat waiting for my answer.

"Leah Velasco," I said reluctantly. "She was our next-door neighbor at our old house."

Olivia stopped chewing. "Leah Velasco!" she exclaimed. "*The* Leah Velasco? Captain of the Northside dance team? You know *that* Leah?"

I sighed. Everyone on the Southside dance team knew about Leah. She was a star. Leah was really the reason Northside had won regionals the last three years running.

"Yep," I answered. "That Leah. We've been friends forever. But I don't know if she'd be too happy about helping me with my pirouettes. It's not like we're on the same team or anything. We're competitors now, not just friends."

Mom frowned. "Oh, Leah's not like that," she said. "Of course she'd be happy to help you!"

Mom's been friends with Leah's mom as long as I've been friends with Leah. Leah's like a second daughter to her. And Mom can never believe anything bad about anyone. She's as loyal as they come.

I decided not to argue. "We'll see," I said. "In the meantime, Olivia and I can practice on our own." My own loyalties were definitely mixed. "Olivia's really good too."

It was almost funny, watching Mom try to decide who to defend. "Of course she is," she said warmly. "I'm sure the two of you will nail those pirouettes."

━━ ━━ ━━ ━━ ━━

Olivia and I practiced for over half an hour, and we didn't nail them—not exactly. But I felt a lot more confident that I *could* nail them, if I kept practicing.

"See you tomorrow morning," Olivia said as she was leaving. "I'll ask my brother if he can give us a ride. He goes early for cross-country practice anyhow. And wait till we tell Camilla that you know Leah Velasco! She'll be wild—Leah's been her archrival since forever!"

My heart sank as I shut the front door. Why did I think that telling Camilla I knew Leah might be a bad idea?

CHAPTER 3

M y alarm went off way too early the next morning. I barely managed to drag myself out of bed and into my dance clothes before Olivia knocked at the front door. I grabbed an energy bar and my water bottle and slipped out of the house.

Camilla got the practice under way at 6:45 exactly. She worked us hard, and I was already feeling sore at the first water break.

"Camilla!" Olivia said excitedly as we

pulled out our water bottles. "Guess who's been friends with Leah Velasco since she was a baby?"

"Who?" Camilla demanded.

"Izzy!" Olivia said. For practically the first time in our friendship, I was annoyed with her. The news wasn't really Olivia's to share.

"You know Leah Velasco?" Camilla asked. "How?"

I explained about how we used to live near each other. "She used to teach me dance routines," I said lamely.

Camilla pounced. "What kind of routines? Do you know what Northside's doing for regionals?"

"No!" I was alarmed. "We just used to fool around, and Leah would show me steps and stuff."

Camilla bit her tongue. I could just imagine her thinking, *If Leah taught you steps, why aren't you a better dancer?*

But that wasn't where Camilla's mind was going. "This could be really good," she said. She grinned at me. "You could find out about Northside's plans for regionals and give us an edge!"

A senior named Jaci picked up on Camilla's idea. "Pick Leah's brain," she said. "Find out what music they're using. You know, are they dancing hop-hop or pom or jazz . . . ?"

"And what their costumes are," added Amelia, another of Camilla's senior friends. "Are they going sexy or chic?"

"Quiz Leah," Camilla said. "Just casually. Tell her how the pirouettes are giving you trouble, and ask what her team's stumbling blocks are. You're smart, Izzy—you could totally pull it off!"

I was feeling really uneasy. Leah might have been acting a little distant since I moved, but she was my friend, and this sounded like spying. Still, Camilla was giving me a real smile, like she and I were friends too.

"Well . . . ," I said. "Leah and I were planning to go to the mall Saturday afternoon. Maybe I could talk to her then."

Camilla laughed. "Better yet, maybe you could just give her a little nudge on the escalator! A broken leg would keep Ms. Stuck-Up out of regionals!"

I tried to laugh along with the rest of the team, but I was horrified. How could Camilla suggest I do something like this to a friend, even as a joke? And Leah wasn't stuck-up!

Something in my face must have given away my true feelings. Camilla exchanged glances with Jaci and Amelia. Then she smiled at me again, warmly and reassuringly.

"I'm just kidding, Izzy," she said. "Bad joke. Now let's get back to practice. By the way, your pirouettes are looking much better today. You must have practiced last night—I'm really impressed at how hard you're working!"

She even gave me a little hug.

So we went back to practicing. This time Camilla had nothing but praise for my dance moves. Part of me felt proud—and relieved. Maybe I really was good enough to dance at regionals with the rest of the team.

But inside I was confused. Was Camilla's praise for real? Or was she just being nice to me so I'd spy on Leah? Was I really supposed to use my friendship to help Southside beat Northside?

CHAPTER 4

Saturday afternoon started with Leah coming by after lunch.

"Hi, Mr. and Mrs. Coleman," she said cheerfully. "I still can't get used to not having you next door. It's just not right!"

Mom beamed at Leah. "I know—it's like old times, having you pop in. Do you want a cookie before you go to the mall? I made peanut butter—your favorite."

"Mmmm!" Leah grabbed two cookies and

threw her arms around Mom. "You're the best—and not just because of your cookies!"

"I can hardly wait till I can drive," I sighed as we settled into Leah's car. "Just six more months till I get my permit!"

Leah and I wandered around the mall for a couple of hours. We talked and window-shopped and tried on makeup. Then we stopped on the second-floor food court for fries and sodas.

"I really love your hair, Izzy," Leah said. "Short suits you—why didn't we ever figure this out before?"

I beamed. "I know! I never knew I had any curl until I chopped off all that weight. But what do you think—should I try some highlights?"

"No," Leah said decisively. "You have natural highlights—why waste your time and money on something you've already got?"

The tone changed when we started to talk about dance team. Leah was the first to bring up the subject.

"So," she said. "How's dance team coming

along? My mom said your mom said you wanted to ask me about something?"

A flash of annoyance at Mom struck me. I could handle my own problems. I know I sounded flustered when I answered Leah.

"Oh, it's nothing really important," I stammered. "I was just having trouble with some of the choreography, and Mom thought maybe you could give me some pointers."

Leah's answer was a little cool. "Probably your own captain would be a better person to ask. Camilla's a good dancer—I'm sure she could help you out."

I felt my cheeks get hot. Did Leah just see me as a competitor? Was being on Southside's dance team going to change our friendship?

"Look, Izzy," Leah said. "I know you're excited to be on Southside's team. But I wouldn't get your hopes up too high about regionals. Northside has the stronger squad—that's all there is to it. Our dancers are more experienced, our team's been around longer than Southside's, we get more money from our school, and we have a professional choreographer who helps us with our routines."

After that, I was really burning. "Northside might be better than Southside," I said. "But that doesn't mean we don't have a chance. We're not going to just roll over and play dead. My mom should never have said anything to yours. I don't need your help!"

"Well, you sure needed it in the past," Leah said. "Don't think I'm going to miss my chance to win regionals again. It's my senior year, and I've worked hard for this!"

There was a moment of awkward silence. We sat the food court table, pushing our french fries around in the ketchup puddle.

Leah was the first to break the silence. "I'm sorry, Izzy," she said. She looked a little embarrassed. "I didn't mean to sound so snotty. Really, I think I'm just sad that we're not on the Northside team together. We've looked forward to that since we were little."

She sighed. "But we're not on the same team. And you're a better dancer than you think. Of course you're going to do your best to kick my butt at regionals." She smiled ruefully. "Just like I'm going to do my best to kick yours. But let's not fight about it. Southside has a good team. With time and practice and your kind of determination, there's no reason you can't win . . . just maybe not this year!"

"We'll see about that," I said. But I was able to say it with a smile of my own.

We dumped our plates and went back out to the mall's main hallway. I think we were both happy to leave the dance conversation behind us.

We paused at the top of the escalator. "Do you have time for a manicure?" I asked. "The Salsa Spa on the first floor is running a two-for-one special this weekend. Should we see if they have a couple of openings?"

"Sure," Leah agreed. "My nails are a mess. I haven't been biting them lately, but that's about all I can say."

I laughed. Since she was little, Leah's been famous for chewing her nails when she's nervous. Over the years we've tried everything to get her to stop. The only thing that really works is getting a manicure. After a mani, Leah says she's so busy admiring her fingernails, she can't bear to bite them.

Leah was about to step on the escalator when a group of middle school boys came tearing past us. A redheaded kid bumped right into Leah. He would have knocked her down the escalator if I hadn't grabbed her arm and pulled her back. Hooting and yelling, the boys raced away without even stopping to see if Leah was all right.

"Brats!" I spat after them. "Are you okay, Leah?"

She nodded, her eyes shooting off sparks. "But I wouldn't have been if you hadn't grabbed me." She gave me a big hug. "Thanks, girl! The manicure's on me!"

I hugged back but kept my eyes on the group of boys racing across the first floor of the mall. Wasn't that redheaded boy Camilla's little brother? I'd seen him a couple of times when he walked over from the middle school to get a ride home with Camilla.

And if it was Camilla's brother, was the shove an accident? I couldn't help remembering what Camilla had said in practice on Thursday. "Maybe you could just give her a little nudge on the escalator!"

Remembering that conversation took some of the fun out of the afternoon.

CHAPTER 5

eah and I didn't stay too late at the mall.
We both had to get ready for dance
performances at school basketball games that
night. Luckily, our teams weren't playing
each other. I didn't want to wreck our newly
mended friendship with that much more
competitiveness.

Southside's gym looked ready to burst
when I got to school. Basketball is a big deal
for us, and the team's doing really well this

year. Of course, as Camilla likes to say, at least some of the team's success is due to the terrific halftime performances we put on. Team spirit is a big part of team success, she stresses—and that's where we come in.

"Everyone's here?" Camilla asked, counting noses. "Okay, listen up. Don't forget—we're here to support our team, but every performance is also good practice for regionals. Let's hit those turns, keep our toes pointed and our leaps big, and work our faces!"

Olivia made a silly face. "It's instant energy!" she said, quoting something our adviser once told us. "Don't just stand there looking smug, give us some expression!"

Trez laughed. "I always feel silly winking or making a pouty face, but the audiences seem to like it."

"More with pom dances than jazz or hip-hop," Jaci said.

"Oh, I don't know," Cate added. "As long as what you're doing matches the movement, being expressive is always important. Even in ballet or tap."

While we talked over our routine for the last time, Southside's cheerleaders got the crowd warmed up. The dance team and cheer squad help each other stir up team spirit. Cheerleaders work the crowd during the game. Then we keep the excitement high through halftime. Some people say dance team members are just cheerleader wannabes, but not at Southside. We work together.

For competitions, the dance team always uses recorded music, but the school band plays for our halftime performances. I love dancing to live music—it's just more fun. I also love our costumes. We have different outfits for different routines, but that night's were my favorite—little black sequined skirts, black ankle boots, and bright yellow sleeveless tops that showed just enough of our midriffs. We wore big yellow flowers in our hair, pinned really tightly so they wouldn't shake loose during any of our spins and jumps.

The night's performance was stellar. The band was on fire and so were we. Our turns were tight, our leaps were big—we were all in sync with each other and definitely "on." Olivia's leg-hold turns were a thing of beauty. And not to brag, but I nailed every one of my triple pirouettes! By the time we hit our perfectly in-sync kick line, the crowd was on its feet, cheering like mad.

Camilla congratulated me after the performance. "Good job, Izzy! I love how you're working those turns!"

I beamed with pleasure. Camilla was being so nice to me!

The basketball team was hot too, and Southside won 47–34. As the crowd was heading out, Olivia and I started packing up our dance bags.

"Do you want to call your parents to pick us up, or should I call mine?" I asked.

"It's my turn—" Olivia started to say.

I looked up from my dance bag. Joel and Eli, two of the guys in the band, were standing next to us. Sometimes they joked around with us during games. Joel was cute, and a good trumpet player, too!

"So what do you think, ladies?" Joel asked, looking right at me. "You've been working hard. It's time to relax a little. Do you want to grab a bite at Taco Shack?"

Did I want to grab a bite at Taco Shack with Joel? Of course I did! He was good looking, he was funny, he was a junior, and he had a car!

I could tell from the way Olivia was smiling up at Eli that she wanted to go too.

"Let me give my parents a call, so they know they don't have to pick us up," I said quickly. I knew Mom and Dad wouldn't mind me going out, as long as I was home by curfew.

And then we were off.

CHAPTER 6

"**A**pologies for the mom-van," Joel said as he held the door open for me. "I'm saving for my own car, but for now, this is the best I can do."

"It's a car!" I said happily. "I can't wait to get my driver's license."

Taco Shack was crowded after the game, but we lucked out and actually got a booth.

"You hold the seats and we'll get the food," Eli said. "Tacos and sweet tea all around?"

It was a fun night. Joel and Eli were easy to talk to, and we did a lot of laughing. I couldn't help noticing some of the other girls at Taco Shack looking at us with envy. Just like I used to watch couples when Olivia and I were there on our own.

I also couldn't help noticing how many kids knew Olivia. She seemed to be casual friends with everyone at Southside. Practically anybody who walked by stopped to say hello.

"You danced really well tonight, Izzy," Joel said. "Did you take dance lessons before you moved here?"

Joel had watched me perform! And he knew I had just moved to Southside district. Maybe he'd been paying attention to me for a while, I thought.

"Thanks," I said. I was feeling a little shy, but Joel's warm smile made me relax. "I've been dancing since I was a little kid, but I never expected to make dance team. I wouldn't even have tried out if it weren't for Olivia!"

"Well, you both looked great out there tonight," Eli said.

When Joel drove us home, he dropped Olivia off first and then walked me up to my door. He didn't exactly kiss me, but he did give me a goofy hug.

"We should do this again," he said.

"Okay," I said. I couldn't help grinning like an idiot. "See you on Monday." And then I slipped inside the house. My first date at Southside was a success!

CHAPTER 7

Everyone was a little groggy at Monday morning's dance practice. We were out of sorts and out of sync. Finally, even Camilla relented.

"Okay, fine—this isn't a good day for any of us," she said. "Let's cut practice short. But I want to see everyone here first thing tomorrow, sharp and focused!"

I was stuffing my dance bag when Camilla came up to me. "Hey, Izzy," she said in her friendliest voice. "Want to come to Pancake Corral with Jaci and Amelia and some of the rest of us?"

I blinked in surprise. I knew that Camilla and her friends sometimes went out for breakfast after the early-morning practices, but I'd never been part of that group.

"We need to do some strategic planning," Camilla said. "And I think it's time we got some fresh ideas. Since you're one of our most promising younger members, we'd like your input."

After that, I was really surprised. Flattered, sure, but confused too. Since when was I one of the team's most promising younger members?

"I don't know," I said. "Would I be back in time for first period?"

"Not to worry," Camilla said breezily. "You have English with Ms. Geiger, right? I'll talk to her if we're late. She's the dance team adviser. She understands about these meetings."

Olivia raised her eyebrows at me: *What's up?* I shrugged. *Don't know!*

Then I turned to Camilla. "Sure," I said. "Pancake Corral sounds good."

Breakfast turned out to be a lot of fun. We squeezed into a booth, everyone laughing and joking.

"Scoot your big butt over," Jaci said to Amelia. "You're squishing Izzy."

Amelia made a face. "I haven't had my coffee yet," she said. "Don't make me kill you."

"That stuff'll stunt your growth," Camilla said. "And you're short enough already."

Ana leaned across the booth to me. "Izzy, you have to try the strawberry granola pancakes," she said. "They're the best!"

The rest of the booth groaned. "You always get those," Berit said. "Don't believe her, Izz. Hash browns and the Denver omelet—that's what you want!"

I laughed. It had been a long time since I'd felt like part of a group. Moving to Southside hadn't been as hard as I'd feared. But except for Olivia, I still didn't have a lot of friends. Sure, I knew people, but not counting for dance team, I didn't really belong anywhere.

By the time high school starts, everyone pretty much has their own crowd. I guess I hadn't realized how much I missed being one of the girls until breakfast in the crowded booth at Pancake Corral.

"Okay," Camilla said once we all had our pancakes and hash browns and eggs. "Here's the deal, Izzy. Our team is in trouble. Even with our bake sales and car washes, we're an expensive club for the school to support. And after this year's budget cuts, Mrs. Nuñez is seriously thinking of cutting off our funding."

Camilla took a big bite of hash browns. "But if we win regionals, we create some noise. We make the school look good, give them something to brag about. We might even attract a sponsor."

I was confused. What was I supposed to do about that, except practice my pirouettes more? Did they think I had connections to a sponsor?

Camilla seemed to read my mind. "Here's where you come in, Izzy. Without Leah Velasco, Northside doesn't have a chance of beating us. For the last three years I've watched Leah steal our trophy from us. This is my last year at Southside, and I'm damned if I'm going to let her do it again."

She leaned over and made serious eye contact. "You know Leah. You can help us take her out of the competition."

Suddenly I was even more confused. "You mean, talk her out of entering? She'd never do that!"

"No, no, of course not! Leah would never stay out of regionals by choice. No—you have to make it so she can't enter."

Jaci took up the pitch. "It doesn't have to be anything too serious, Izzy. Go to the mall again. Jostle Leah when she's wearing those high platform sandals she likes, so she gets an ankle sprain." Jaci looked toward Camilla, who gave her a slight nod.

Amelia leaned in closer to me. "Or remember that ice skater from years ago? The one who cut her competitor's leg so she couldn't skate? Maybe you could invite Leah to go to the rink with you, practice turns and leaps, and accidentally graze her. Just enough for a few stitches—and no regionals."

I looked around the booth. Everyone was watching me expectantly. I felt sick to my stomach. They wanted me to hurt Leah? These were the friendly girls who made me feel so welcome?

I didn't want to lose that feeling of belonging. I needed friends, needed to feel as if I fit in at Southside. But could I really do something so evil to Leah? After all, she was my friend too. But then I recalled our conversation at the mall. We were friends outside of regionals, sure. But during the competition, we'd put that on hold. I looked down at my plate of food, unable to answer.

"Never mind, Izzy," Camilla said soothingly. "I don't want you to do anything you don't want to. Leah's your friend. She's probably been helping you get ready for competition. I figure she's the one who's been coaching you on your pirouettes. You probably feel as loyal to her as she does to you."

I felt my cheeks burning. Leah hadn't been coaching me. In fact, she pretty much refused to help me when I out and out asked her. Instead, she said she was going to do her best to kick my butt. Maybe she wasn't the friend I wanted her to be?

Camilla patted my hand. "It really is okay, Izzy," she said. "We can beat Northside even with Leah Velasco performing. Now, your pancakes are getting cold—eat!"

She turned the conversation back to dance team and school gossip. I picked at my soggy food, less eager to talk than I had been before.

CHAPTER 8

I couldn't help worrying about what Camilla and the other girls had said about Leah. But as the week went by, I relaxed a little. Camilla didn't mention Leah to me again. She seemed totally focused on improving our own team's performance.

Anyway, I had plenty to think about with school, my own dancing and, more recently, Joel. We started having lunch and walking to classes together. And since there wasn't a home basketball game on Saturday, we went with Olivia and Eli to see a movie and grab some pizza. Thinking about a cute guy who was close to being my boyfriend helped distract me from worring so much about Camilla.

Joel teased me as we stepped out of the theater. "Earth to Izzy. Was the movie that good?"

I flushed. The movie had been good, but that wasn't what I was thinking about. At least, not exactly. The movie was about two friends who grew apart, then came together again when one of them got sick. Instead of taking my mind off my problems with Leah and Camilla, the film just made me think about them more. My life seemed to have become much more complicated since I made dance team at Southside. And complicated did not equal fun.

I looked at Joel, who had a puzzled expression. I didn't want to spoil this evening, and I tried to shake myself out of my funk. "I'm just deciding what kind of pizza I want," I said with a laugh.

"I like a girl who's always thinking about her stomach," Joel said. He took my hand and squeezed it—and then didn't let go.

The warm pressure of Joel's hand made me forget about Camilla. A date with a cute boy was a lot more fun than thinking about sabotaging Northside's dance team!

— — — — —

The fun lasted until Monday morning. When we got to school for our early-morning practice, we were stopped cold. One whole side of the gym was covered with graffiti. Really mean graffiti, and it was all about the dance team. Each of us was mentioned by name, and the things we were called made me blush.

"Northside rocks—Southside sucks," Olivia read, as we stood there gaping. It was the cleanest thing written.

By noon, the whole school was talking about the graffiti. Rumors flew, and most of them were about how Leah Velasco was responsible.

"They found her student ID card behind the gym," Ana said. "And I heard people at Northside found paint and receipts from Home Depot in her locker!"

"She's going to be disqualified from regionals," Jaci said smugly. "Disfiguring public property and unsportsmanlike behavior. She'll probably get kicked off the dance team. Maybe even suspended from school."

I couldn't believe it. Leah would never do anything like that! Or would she? Was she just bluffing with all her talk about how Northside was the stronger team? Did Leah really think Southside was too much of a threat?

I thought about what she'd said at the mall: *Southside has a good team. With time and practice and your kind of determination, there's no reason you can't win . . .*

Could Leah be capable of trashing the Southside gym? I wondered.

Principal Nuñez and Ms. Geiger both showed up at our after-school practice. They looked grim.

Mrs. Nuñez got right to the point. "As you know, we had an act of vandalism over the weekend. Someone defaced the gym with some pretty nasty graffiti about the dance team."

"I know rumors have been flying," Ms. Geiger added. "The general understanding seems to be that Northside is responsible, and specifically their dance team captain, Leah Velasco. It's true that Leah's student ID was found near the gym. It's also true that a can of paint and some receipts were found in her locker."

"What isn't true is that Leah had anything to do with the graffiti," Mrs. Nuñez said. "She was in Austin with her family for the entire weekend. We've confirmed this. There's no way she could have been involved."

Ms. Geiger looked even grimmer than before. "Which means the ID card and paint were planted to make Leah look guilty. That sounds like someone at Southside is responsible."

A moment of uncomfortable silence followed her words. Camilla didn't look at anyone.

"I would hate to think that any of our students could sink this low," Mrs. Nuñez said sternly. "This is an ugly, ugly act, and we're

going to do our best to get to the bottom of it.
To this end, I would like anyone who knows
anything—*anything*—about this to come to
me or Ms. Geiger. Whatever you say will be
kept confidential."

There was another uncomfortable pause.

"All right," Ms. Geiger said with a sigh.
"You know where to find us. Now get on with
your practice. We all want to win regionals—
but we'll win cleanly or not at all!"

CHAPTER 9

For the rest of the week, things were tense at school. Nobody had been able to prove anything about the graffiti incident. I couldn't help suspecting Camilla, Jaci, and Amelia, but I didn't say anything. How could I? I didn't have any proof, just the memory of a conversation in a booth at Pancake Corral. A conversation that didn't include anything about graffiti.

Leah was furious. She called me practically

the minute school was out on Monday. "What the hell is going on at that school of yours?" she asked.

"I don't know!" I said. "It's awful!"

We talked for a while, but I don't know what I could have said to fix things. Somebody at my school had done a horrible thing to Leah. She was mad. She had a right to be.

On Saturday night we had another basketball halftime performance. I don't know if it was the graffiti, but we weren't at the top of our game. Cate—who never messes up—fell during her jazz layout, and that tripped up Jaci and Amelia. The two of them were so mad at Cate that they came in late with their wing approaches, and all three girls missed their double syncopated pull-back. By then we were all out of sync with the music, and we never really got our timing back. As for my triple pirouettes—well, the less said, the better.

After halftime show ended, I could see Camilla was furious.

"This better *never* happen again," she spat as she shoved that night's outfit into her sports bag. "I'll see you all at Monday practice. 6:45 A.M. sharp, and *no* tardies or absences!" She stormed out of the gym, not waiting around to watch the basketball team play, which she always insists that we do.

The game was a heart-stopper. Olivia and I sat near the band. For most of the last quarter, we were on our feet. The lead went back and forth between Southside and Eastlake. Southside's cheerleaders did their best, and Olivia and I cheered our hardest. With seconds remaining on the clock, Southside was ahead two points.

"We've got it!" Olivia screamed as she clutched me. We watched our center take control of the ball, sprint down the court— and trip.

Nobody pushed him. It wasn't a foul. It was just awful, terrible luck. He caught himself and lurched upright, but by then he'd lost control of the ball. An Eastlake point guard was there to grab it, pivot, and shoot a three-pointer just as the buzzer went off. The game ended with Southside losing 77–76.

Joel, Eli, Olivia, and I were quiet when we went out for pizza afterwards.

"Well, that was a heartbreaker of a game," Joel said glumly.

"And we stank in our halftime show," Olivia said.

"Oh, you weren't so bad," Eli said. "There was just that little mix-up when Cate fell."

"It was a lot more than that," Olivia replied. "Camilla's out for blood."

"She's pretty intense," Joel said. "We're neighbors, and I've seen her practicing. She really wants this dance team thing to succeed."

I sighed. Didn't we all want the dance team to succeed? The difference was in what steps we were willing to take to make it happen.

CHAPTER 10

After pizza, everyone decided to make it an early night. The fact that Joel gave me a for-real good-night kiss helped boost my spirits, but I wished I'd been in a better mood to appreciate it.

It's just as well I was rested on Sunday. Mom had invited Leah and her parents over for a backyard barbecue. I'd need all my energy to face Leah. The plans had been made before the graffiti incident, but Mom and Dad were especially keen on having the Velascos over after all the trouble.

"I can't believe anyone would do something so mean!" Mom sputtered when she first heard. "Dance team is supposed to be fun. If the competitions can't be about skill and challenge, what's the point? Winning by cheating isn't winning at all!"

Leah got right to the point when she and her family arrived. She gave my mom and dad a quick hug, then grabbed my arm and steered me to the backyard.

"Well?" she demanded. "Have you found out who did that graffiti yet? And how did they get my ID or my locker combination? You'd better tell me everything you know, Izzy!"

I couldn't blame Leah for still being mad about the graffiti. But I resented her thinking that I might have had anything to do with it.

"I don't know anything!" I said. "I told you, I was as shocked as anyone when I got to school on Monday. We were all surprised!"

I felt a little guilty when I added that last part. Somebody wasn't surprised. And I felt even guiltier when I thought that I might know who that somebody was

Leah didn't look convinced. "Oh, come on, Izzy. People talk. You must have heard something by now. Or are you just trying to protect your precious dance team?"

"No!" I was really stung. "Why would I do anything to hurt you? You're my friend!"

I felt guiltier and more confused than ever. Was I telling Leah the truth? Was I hurting her by not going to Mrs. Nuñez or Ms. Geiger with my suspicions? Or would that just be smearing Camilla and her friends, since I didn't know anything for sure? What about being innocent until proven guilty?

I tried again to calm Leah down. "The principal and our coach are trying as hard as they can to find out who's responsible. Really, Leah. And the other girls on the team are as upset as I am."

That was at least partly true. Olivia was horrified, and girls like Trez and Cate seemed genuinely shocked too. It made me feel a little better to know that not everyone was out to get Leah.

Leah looked less angry and more sad. "You can't imagine how I felt, coming back from Austin to find people believed I might have done that graffiti. Even kids I thought were my friends were wondering!"

I began to feel sorrier and sorrier. Even I had wondered if she could have been the guilty one.

"Oh, Leah," I said. I reached over and gave her a tight hug. She was stiff at first but then loosened up. "I can't imagine. But if I ever find out who did this and tried to make people think it was you, I'll break their legs. Honest!"

Leah sniffed. "Okay, then. But just be sure you call me first, so I can help."

We had a little weepy moment while she hugged me back. I felt more conflicted than ever. Was someone really trying to hurt Leah? How far would they go?

CHAPTER 11

"**C**an you believe regionals are only two weeks away?" Olivia asked at our after-school dance practice on Monday.

"No!" I said. "I feel like I know our routine pretty well, but I'm not perfect on the switch leaps in the second chorus."

"It's the leg-hold turns that I'm worried about," Olivia confided to me. "I'm afraid Camilla's going to take me off turns if I don't pick up the pace."

"Oh, she won't do that!" I said. I could sympathize with Olivia. I think everyone on the team felt pressure about the turn combinations. Sometimes dance captains adapt the choreography if all the girls can't hit the turns consistently. They give the weaker girls something else to do while the rest of the team turns. This takes away from the look of the dance, since everyone's not doing the same thing, but it's still better than having someone fall out of her turns. Camilla, though, wanted everyone to keep in sync.

"Girls!" Camilla's voice was sharp. "Enough chatter! Opening formation, please!"

From then on it was all work, no play. As ever, Camilla didn't miss a thing. "Ana—point your toes! Cate—your hands are flopping around like a couple of dead fish! Olivia—those leg-hold turns are looking better, but still not sharp enough! In fact, you all need to work on getting those leg-hold turns synchronized! They're way too sloppy!"

After an hour, everyone was sweaty and breathless. But it was a good kind of tired, and for the first time I started to think that maybe we really would be ready to compete in two weeks.

Apparently Camilla agreed with me. "Okay, that's enough," she announced. She allowed herself a little smile. "Don't get too excited, but you guys are actually beginning to look like a dance team. Keep up the good work, and I might even take you to regionals!"

Everyone laughed as they gathered up their stuff. I made a snap decision. I had something to say to Camilla, and I figured I might as well take advantage of her good mood.

"Wait for me," I told Olivia. "I have to talk to Camilla."

Confronting Camilla wasn't as hard as I'd thought. Probably because I didn't give myself time to think about what I was going to say.

"Hey, Izzy," Camilla said. "You're looking good out there!" She sounded perfectly friendly and normal, and her smile looked genuine.

I didn't let myself get distracted. "Camilla," I blurted out. "Did you have anything to do with the graffiti?"

Camilla's smile disappeared in a heartbeat. "Are you accusing me of vandalism, Izzy?" she asked.

"I'm just wondering," I said stubbornly. "After what we talked about at the Pancake Corral and all."

"I don't know what you mean," Camilla said in her steeliest voice. "I certainly never talked about any graffiti!"

My courage was starting to fail me. "No," I said uncertainly. "But the other stuff..."

Camilla zipped up her dance bag. "I don't know what you're talking about," she repeated. "But I do know that team loyalty is as important as dance moves. If you want to accuse me of something, do it in front of the whole team, okay? Let's see what they think about a rookie freshman calling the team captain a vandal and a liar."

Camilla had me. She knew I'd never say anything to the rest of the team. Not two weeks before regionals, not when I didn't have any proof.

"Well?" Camilla asked. "Are we done here?"

I nodded meekly. Yes, we were done. I watched Camilla walk away. Her head was up, her shoulders were back. She wasn't afraid of anything I could do to her. And why should she be? I was just a freshman—and a very confused one at that.

CHAPTER 12

"What was that all about?" Olivia asked when I joined her by the bleachers.

"I'll tell you later," I said. At that moment, I just wanted to get out of the gym.

Olivia nodded. "Look," she said, nudging me.

I looked. Joel and Eli were standing in the gym doorway. They saw us and waved, then came over to where we were standing.

"Hey," Joel said. "Band practice just ended. Want to grab a taco?"

"Sure," Olivia said easily. "Izzy?"

"Absolutely." I had spent enough time keeping my worries bottled up. I had to talk to someone.

I waited till we were tucked into the booth at Taco Shack before I got started. I explained about everything—the incident at the mall escalator, the breakfast at Pancake Corral, my suspicions about Camilla and the graffiti.

Olivia looked shocked. "I can't believe Camilla would do anything like this!" she said. "I mean, I know dance team means everything to her, but this goes too far. Are you sure you didn't misunderstand, Izzy?"

"I heard what I heard," I said. Why wouldn't Olivia believe me?

Eli shook his head. "There's got to be some other explanation. The thing at the mall was probably just an accident. You know how crazy little kids can get when they're running around in a gang. And Camilla and the others were probably just joking at that breakfast."

Joel looked troubled. "I don't know," he said. "I live on Camilla's block, and I've known her all my life. She's always been hardcore about getting what she wants. Not mean, exactly—but she doesn't let anything stop her once she's made up her mind. If Camilla wants to win regionals and she thinks Leah Velasco is standing in her way . . ."

"But how could she have had anything to do with the graffiti?" Olivia argued. "Whoever did that had to know someone at Northside. They had to break into Leah's locker and steal her ID. "

Joel looked even more troubled. "Camilla's cousin Alex goes to Northside," he said. "Alex's kind of a wild dude. He's been in trouble at school before. Not big stuff, just cheating on tests, skipping school, getting caught drinking at dances, stuff like that. Alex doesn't have a whole lot of school spirit. I could see him thinking it would be fun, getting someone like Leah in trouble."

Olivia shook her head. "I'm sorry, Izzy, but I still can't believe it," she said. "There's got to be another explanation."

"I hope so," I said. Olivia was supposed to be my friend, and friends are supposed to stick together. Yet there she was, siding with Camilla instead of me. What kind of friend was that?

"I'm sure of it," Olivia said firmly. "Dance team means everything to Camilla. She'd do anything to win regionals, but not if it meant getting the team in trouble. And deliberately hurting Leah would definitely get the team in trouble. After all the work Camilla's put into this team—it was practically dead when she came in as a freshman. If it weren't for Camilla, Southside wouldn't even have a dance team! She wouldn't risk everything in her last year!"

I hoped Olivia was right.

CHAPTER 13

Olivia knew I was upset with her. I avoided her at school for a couple days while I sorted things out.

I tried to put myself in her position— would I believe a new friend, a friend making pretty wild accusations, over the senior dance team captain who was responsible for getting me a place on the squad?

Olivia made it hard to stay angry for long. She was waiting at my locker when I got out of biology Tuesday afternoon.

"Hey, girl," she said. "I know you're mad at me for not believing you about Leah and Camilla. I guess I don't blame you. It's just . . . the idea of Camilla trying to hurt Leah is just such a weird idea, like something you'd see in a movie. Not like anything that happens in real life."

I couldn't help agreeing with her. "I know," I said. "But if you'd heard Camilla and you knew Leah . . ."

"Exactly," Olivia said. "I didn't hear Camilla, and I don't know Leah. But we could fix at least part of that—why don't you introduce me to her? We've been friends ever since you moved, and I've never even met your best friend from your old neighborhood! Can we do something this weekend? Go shopping? Get lunch?"

I considered it while we waited at the bus stop. People jostled all around, talking and laughing, making plans. All the noise and commotion made it hard to think, but really, what was there to think about? Why shouldn't

Olivia and Leah get to know each other? They were both important people in my life. And maybe if Olivia met Leah, she'd understand why Camilla made me worry. I could use Olivia's support. At the very least, she and Leah would probably get along.

"Sure," I said. "But let's do something other than shopping. How about a bike ride? Leah lives near a forest preserve with great bike paths."

"Sounds like fun," Olivia said.

"I'll call Leah tonight," I decided. "My dad can drive us over to her house. We already have bike racks on our car."

"Perfect!" Olivia said.

Camilla and Jaci hung behind us as we crowded on the bus. Had they heard me making plans to see Leah? They certainly were whispering together. I couldn't hear everything they were saying, but one phrase stood out: "Operation Bring Her Down, part three." What did that mean?

CHAPTER 14

Saturday was gorgeous. Warm and sunny, with just the hint of a breeze. Leah came running out when Dad dropped Olivia and me off at her house. She'd seemed really happy when I called to suggest the bike ride, and she gave both me and Olivia big hugs.

"Hey, you two!" she said. "I'm glad to finally meet you, Olivia. I miss Izzy so much, but it's good to know she's got a friend like you."

Whew. Leah was back to her old super-friendly self. I crossed my fingers and hoped we'd be able to avoid any dance team talk. We took a few minutes to pump up our tires, adjust our bike seats, and make sure our helmets fit.

Leah was ready first. "I'm just going to ride up and down the street a little," she called as she coasted down the driveway. "I'll wait for you at—yikes! Help!"

I looked up just in time to see a passing car slam on its brakes while Leah veered off the driveway onto the grass, where she crashed in a heap.

"Leah!" Olivia and I ran over to her. "Are you okay? What happened?"

"My brakes didn't work!" she said. "I was trying to slow down for that car, but they didn't catch!"

The driver rolled down her window and stuck out her head. "You all right?" she called.

Leah waved. "I'm fine," she called back. "Problem with my brakes."

The woman shook her head. "Be careful! Better get those checked out!"

While I helped Leah up, Olivia examined her bike. "Look," she said. "Your brake quick-release cable's undone."

I'm not much of a bike expert. "What does that mean?" I asked. "How did it happen?"

"It's this little lever here," Leah said, pointing. "It could have come undone on its own," she added. "But it's never happened before."

"Could someone have been trying to adjust it or anything, and maybe forgot to hook it up again?" Olivia asked

Leah shook her head. "I don't think so," she said. "This is my bike. I'm the only one who ever rides it."

I felt a shiver go down my spine. Could someone have undone the brake release deliberately? I remembered Camilla and Jaci standing behind me at the bus stop when Olivia and I were making our bike-riding plans. What was it they'd said? "Operation Bring Her Down, part three."

"You lock your bike up in the garage at night, right?" I said, trying to sound casual.

"Not usually," Leah said. "I just leave it in the backyard, inside the gate. Why?"

I hesitated. "Oh, I was just wondering if maybe some kids were out goofing around and thought it would be cool to mess with your bike." I sounded pretty lame, even to myself.

Leah looked at me sharply. "Kids?" she said. "Or some of your dance team vandals?"

Her voice rose. "You think someone did this deliberately?"

Olivia and I exchanged glances. "No," I said slowly. "I honestly can't imagine anyone doing something like this. You could have been really hurt!"

"*Did* you get hurt?" Olivia asked. "Did you skin your knees, pull any muscles?"

Leah shook her head. "I'm fine," she said shortly. "But if I find out anyone did this on purpose . . ."

I was quiet for a minute. "Do you still want to go for a ride?" I asked. "We could do something else if you want. Or we could just go home . . ."

"No!" Leah said. "Don't go home. Probably I just bumped the brake release when I was fixing my seat. I can't believe it could have happened any other way. I'm not hurt, and I don't want to spoil our afternoon. We don't get to see each other enough, Izzy. I really don't want this whole dance competition to wreck things!"

I breathed a sigh of relief. I didn't want the competition to wreck things either. For the rest of the day, we didn't say another word about dance team.

CHAPTER 15

Before I knew it, regionals weekend had arrived! Dad drove Olivia and me to Austin early Saturday morning. Olivia's parents would bring Mom over later in the afternoon, to see our performance.

"I'm so nervous I could barely eat breakfast," Olivia said as we picked her up.

"Me too," I said. "Do you think Cate and Trez and Camilla still get butterflies?"

"Probably," Olivia said. "Just maybe not

as bad." She held up her hands. "What do you think of my manicure?"

"Whew! For a minute I thought you'd gotten color. Camilla would've killed you if you had!"

Olivia tossed her head. "I'm nervous, not crazy," she said. "I know we need naked nails for performance. And I like French manicures better than color anyhow."

I did too. But I'd done my own nails, using my palest neutral polish. Camilla was a stickler about us not having clashing colors during performances.

"Can you believe we're really going to regionals?" I asked. "It doesn't seem real. Wasn't it, like, yesterday that we were auditioning for the team?"

"I was just about as nervous then," Olivia giggled. "Think how far we've come, Izzy! It's not just your pirouettes that have improved. Everything about you as a dancer is more polished and, well, just *better* than last fall."

That was true. I *was* a much better

dancer than I'd been six months before. But in the weeks before regionals, I'd been so worried about the whole Camilla-Leah thing, I hadn't really been thinking about my own dancing. I felt a spurt of anger. It wasn't fair, having my first time at a big competition spoiled! I wished I could enjoy the day without having to worry about what Camilla might or might not be planning for Leah, or about whether Leah and I would still be friends at the end!

"Thanks, Olivia," I said. "You've gotten a lot better too. Of course, you were always a better dancer than I am!"

Before we knew it, Dad was pulling up to the campus where regionals was being held.

"Break a leg, girls!" Dad said cheerily as he dropped us off at the big university field house. I've never liked that expression, but my dad used to be in plays in college, and there's no stopping him from saying it.

"You bet, Mr. Coleman," Olivia answered. She thinks he's funny—but then, he's not her father.

"Thanks for the ride, Dad," I said. I leaned in the car window and gave him a quick kiss. "And if there are any broken legs, I'm holding you responsible!"

CHAPTER 16

Things were crazy inside the field house. We found Southside's designated corner of the dressing room and dumped our stuff. Every girl was responsible for her own outfit and makeup, and Ms. Geiger was there to be sure nobody had forgotten anything.

"Olivia, Izzy," Ms. Geiger said, checking off her clipboard. "Leggings, tunic, headband, shoes. Here—you each get a wristlet to match the headband. Put it with the rest of your costume on the rack over there. And you're good with makeup?"

We were. We hung up our outfits and then squeezed onto the bench in front of the long mirrors. Everything seemed too real as we put on our eyeliner, mascara, blush, lip gloss, and sparkly turquoise eye shadow to match our tunics.

I liked the new regionals outfit almost as much as the black-and-yellow halftime clothes. We wore tight black leggings, soft black ballet slippers, and flowing electric turquoise tunics. Judges at regionals don't like anything too sexy, but the tunic's dipping neckline and fitted waist added a touch of flashiness.

"Okay, now I'm officially nervous," Olivia announced. "Is it too late to drop out?"

Trez was sitting next to her. "You'll be fine, Olivia," she laughed. "You look gorgeous! And once you get onstage and hear the music, everything will fall into place."

"Do you promise?" I asked, smoothing my eye shadow.

"I promise," said Camilla, coming up behind us. "This is what we've been working for all year! A little bit of nerves is a good thing. You need that extra adrenaline!"

She actually gave Olivia and me quick hugs. I guess Camilla knew that for performance day, encouragement was better than criticism.

"Izzy!" I turned to see Leah hurrying towards me. "I'm glad I found you! I wanted to say good luck at your first regionals!" She dropped her dance bag on the bench next to me and gave me a huge hug. "Ooh—I like your eyeshadow!"

Camilla smiled at Leah and me. "Do you want to show Leah your costume, Izzy?" she asked.

"Sure!" I said, a little surprised. Usually Camilla's so top secret about anything involving regionals. But I guess by that point, it was too late for secrets.

"Thanks, Camilla," Leah said. "That's nice of you."

As Leah oohed over the slinky, glittery turquoise tunic and shiny black leggings, I glanced back at Camilla. She was hovering over Leah's dance bag. Wait—was she actually fiddling with it? In the crowded dressing room, I couldn't be sure.

Camilla picked up my bag, then Olivia's, and moved them so that she'd have room on the bench to sit and apply her makeup. Maybe my suspicions were getting the best of me, I thought. Camilla probably just moved Leah's bag for the same reason.

"Okay, Izzy, I've got to get ready myself," Leah said. "What was it your dad always used to tell me? Break a leg!"

We both laughed. Seeing Leah calmed me down. I'd watched her perform so many times that talking to her for a bit made everything seem almost normal.

Camilla watched Leah leave. Then I saw her give Amelia a tiny, secret little thumbs-up sign. What was going on?

I didn't have much time to wonder. "Somebody, help!" Olivia wailed. "My hair's so frizzy! I can't get my ponytail right!"

"Can you help her, Izzy?" Camilla said.

"You're always so good with hair."

Flattered, I turned my attention to Olivia. Since I keep my hair short, I don't need to spend much time getting it ready. Throughout the season, I'd helped Olivia and Cate get their ponytails sleek and smooth. But I never knew Camilla had noticed.

"Relax, Olivia," I said soothingly. "You just need more hairspray. Here—let me!"

When I was finished, Jaci asked me to do her hair too. In the rush of helping the other girls and finishing my makeup, I forgot all about the dance bags. I just wanted our squad to be perfect for regionals!

CHAPTER 17

I don't think I've ever been as nervous as I was while we got into position and waited for the judges to give us the go-ahead sign. Waiting is the worst!

But Trez was right. Once the music started and we started dancing, it was great! We had chosen a sassy jazz routine with lots of big leaps and flashy turns. We started out in a single straight line, with our backs to the audience, tapping our toes back and forth to the music's beat. Then we turned to face the crowd, three at a time, in perfect synchronization. After that, we moved into our opening formation.

The crowd loved our routine. It gave us lots of cheering support as we moved from one formation to another. And we deserved it, if I do say so myself! We were tight and in sync, and our energy levels were out of this world. Everyone hit their turns, our leaps were huge, and we didn't have to pretend-act to get our excitement across to the audience.

By the time we hit our final turn combination, people in the audience were flashing their own jazz hands back at us.

Afterwards, we all clustered around, congratulating each other. Even Camilla was beaming. "That was the best ever," she said, throwing her arms around whoever she could find. "You guys are stellar!"

Once we were finished, we could relax and watch the other routines. Some good teams had shown up to compete, but I didn't think any of them performed as well as we did. I was feeling pretty excited about our chances of winning—until Northside came up. They were the last team to perform, and they were good. Really, really good. Maybe not better than we were—but close.

Everyone from Southside got quiet as we watched them. The Northside girls were dressed all in black. They performed a hip-hop number that was as fast and edgy as it was fun to watch.

Hip-hop isn't as technically difficult as jazz. It's more about style and keeping the audience entertained. But Northside totally nailed its number. The dancers stayed close to the ground and hit their tricks hard and fast. They moved effortlessly from windmills to hand-stalls to kip-ups, and their freezes were textbook perfect. The crowd went wild. It was pretty clear that the real competition was going to be between us and Northside.

The girls from Northside were just taking their bows when I saw Camilla slip away from the group. I didn't think anything about it—

she probably just had to go to the bathroom. But then I saw her talking to one of the officials. The two of them headed toward the dressing room.

And then everything blew up.

CHAPTER 18

N orthside's team had barely made it off the stage when one of the judges announced that there was a problem. Final scores would be delayed. We were to return to the changing area and wait for further instructions.

"What's going on?" hissed Olivia as we were herded back to the dressing room.

"I have no idea!" I said. "Something bad, that's for sure!"

My heart sank when we went into the

dressing room. Leah was arguing with two of the judges, tears streaming down her face. One of the judges was holding Leah's dance bag. He had something in his hand—it looked like a pill bottle.

Pretty soon we heard the official explanation. Performance-enhancing drugs had been found in Leah's dance bag. Instant grounds for disqualification.

The room buzzed with talk following the announcement. I searched the crowd for Camilla. Sure enough, she was standing by an official, the same one she'd gone to talk to in the auditorium. Her face didn't give anything away. But I knew what had happened. I just knew. And when Camilla came back to our group, I lit into her.

"Camilla! Did you put those pills in Leah's dance bag? I saw you fiddling with it when I was showing Leah my costume!"

The team was shocked into silence.

"Izzy!" Olivia whispered. "What are you talking about?"

"I'm talking about Camilla playing dirty

tricks to get Leah disqualified!"

I was sure I was right. Words tumbled out of me. The escalator, the breakfast at Pancake Corral, the graffiti, the bike brakes—all the ways I was sure Camilla and her friends had been trying to get Leah out of competition.

Camilla let me finish. "I don't know what you're talking about, Izzy," she said. "Honestly, you sound a little crazy. I'm sorry your precious friend Leah isn't so perfect. But there's no reason to blame me because Leah takes drugs."

The other girls looked shocked.

"Izzy?" Cate said. "Camilla's right. This does sound a little . . . far-fetched."

"But it's true!" I insisted. "Camilla wanted me to make it so Leah couldn't compete. She was willing to hurt Leah to win regionals. I'm going to tell Ms. Geiger!"

Even Olivia looked troubled. "But Izzy, you don't have any proof! You're just going to stir up trouble and make everything worse. We need this win! Our whole team might be lost without it!"

I looked at the rest of the dance team. I could tell that nobody believed me. And really, why would they have? I didn't have any proof.

But I didn't care. Even if I couldn't get anyone else to believe me, not even Olivia, I owed it to Leah to try to set things straight. I knew—with no doubt—that Leah would never use illegal drugs.

So I marched over to Ms. Geiger and spilled out everything. First, she looked confused. Then she looked concerned. Then she looked sad and grim.

Things happened pretty fast after that. Officials and team advisers went team by team, searching bags and backpacks for drugs or other "incriminating evidence."

And they found it. Camilla had an identical bottle of pills in her backpack. At first, she denied knowing anything about the drugs.

"They must have been planted!" Camilla spat. "Probably by Leah Velasco!"

"Well, Camilla," said Ms. Geiger. "You got the steroids for something. If they weren't to plant on Leah, were they for your personal use?"

Camilla drew herself up proudly. "No! I don't need steroids. I'm a dancer! I don't abuse my body! I work for what I do!"

And then she broke down and owned up to everything. The mall, the graffiti, even the bike brakes. When none of those worked, she got her cousin Alex to use his connections to get some steroids for her. The idea was that Camilla would slip one bottle into Leah's dance bag and one bottle into her backpack. But in the end, she was only able to get the pills into the dance bag. She held onto the second bottle as insurance, in case she could sneak it into the backpack later.

Camilla's confession was enough. Southside was disqualified from the competition, and Northside was awarded first prize at regionals for their fourth year running.

"The sad thing is that you girls had a really good chance of winning this year," Ms. Geiger told us. "I don't know what the final decision would have been, but I've been to enough competitions to know that you and Northside were neck and neck."

She sighed. "But the worst part, of course, is what Camilla felt driven to do. Trust me, I know how hard she's worked for dance team these past four years. It's just a terrible, terrible shame that she couldn't trust your skill, your determination, and your hard work to win the trophy."

And that was how regionals ended for us.

CHAPTER 19

W e were a pretty subdued group as we changed out of our regionals outfits and gathered up our dance bags. The rest of the team seemed to be avoiding my eyes. Even Olivia didn't seem to know what to say.

Leah did, though. She came barreling through the crowd and gave me a tight hug. "Thank you, Izzy," she said. "I'm sorry if I ever, ever doubted you. You're a true friend. *And* a good dancer. When all this blows over and Southside gets on its feet again, you'll win a regionals trophy. I'm sure of it!"

I laughed a little shakily. "Somehow, wanting to win seems a little dangerous right now."

"No!" Leah said. "Winning legitimately is the best feeling. You deserve that feeling, Izzy!"

She hurried off to join her family, and I was left with my own team again.

Cate was the first one to break the silence. "This is too hard to believe, Izzy," she said. "I don't know who to be madder at, you or Camilla!"

Jaci snorted. "I do," she said. "And it's not Camilla! We deserved to win this! We would have too, if it weren't for Izzy!"

A troubled look crossed Trez's face. "Or if it weren't for Camilla," she said. "I for one don't want to win by cheating. Why couldn't Camilla have believed in us as much as she made us think she did?"

"Why couldn't Izzy have minded her own business?" said Amelia.

Cate gave Amelia a steely look. "Maybe you should have minded *your* own business," she said. "It sounds like Camilla's not the only one who has something to apologize for!"

I couldn't keep silent any longer. "I really am sorry for all of this," I said. "I never wanted to ruin our chances. Maybe it would be better for everyone if I just resigned from the team."

"Yes!" said Jaci and Amelia.

"No," said Trez. "That's no solution." She laughed faintly, but it wasn't like she thought anything was funny. "Right now we don't even know if we have a dance team for you to resign from! We'll have to wait to see what Ms. Geiger and Mrs. Nuñez say on Monday."

CHAPTER 20

Sunday was a long day. I spent it at home with my family. Mom and Dad were especially nice to me, but all I wanted to do was sleep and try to forget the whole mess. I didn't even see Olivia. I had no idea whether or not she even wanted to be my friend anymore.

I didn't feel any better by Monday. For once, Mom and Dad let me stay home from school. I slept most of the day, so maybe I really was sick. I spent my time away from

Southside High lying on the couch in the family room and flipping from channel to channel on TV.

As soon as school was out, Olivia called. "Joel and Eli are here. Can we come over?" she asked.

I didn't feel like I could blame Olivia for questioning my suspicions about Camilla. They were pretty wild, after all. We don't expect people we know—our friends—to act, well, like TV bad guys.

"Sure," I said. "I'd like that."

Olivia let out a sigh of relief. "Oh, Izzy," she wailed over the phone. "I'm so sorry I didn't believe you from the beginning. I should have trusted you."

"It's okay," I said. And it was, too. "Nothing Camilla did was the kind of stuff you'd expect from someone you look up to, someone you want to call a friend."

Joel and Eli wanted to know all the details when they arrived with Olivia.

"It was Camilla's little brother who bumped Leah at the mall," I said. "And her cousin Alex helped her and Amelia and Jaci do the graffiti, just like you thought, Joel."

"Camilla, Jaci, and Amelia tinkered with Leah's bike brakes," Olivia added. "They heard us talking about going biking. They drove by Leah's house the Friday before, and Jaci snuck in to mess with the brake cable."

"I kind of have to hand it to Camilla," I said. "She confessed to everything, but she didn't drag in Jaci or Amelia."

"But then they confessed on their own," Olivia added. "They didn't leave Camilla hanging."

Loyalty is a funny thing.

"So what happens now?" Joel asked.

"Camilla, Jaci, and Amelia are suspended for two weeks. Leah's family doesn't want to pursue criminal charges, but Camilla and Alex will still have to deal with the illegal drugs stuff," Olivia said.

"And dance team's disbanded for the rest of the year," I said sadly. "Ms. Geiger said they'd have to review everything before they decide if we can perform and compete next year."

"I bet you will," Joel said encouragingly. "It's not like the rest of you did anything wrong. And you were so good at regionals!"

"You were there?" I said, surprised.

"Of course we were!" Eli answered. "Where else would we be?"

Suddenly I felt a little better. "Maybe with someone like Cate or Trez as captain, Mrs. Nuñez will let us keep going," I said. "Most of the team didn't know anything about what Camilla was up to. We still have three years to win regionals!"

"And nail my leg-hold turns," Olivia said.

I smiled. "And my triple pirouettes!"

About the Author

Charnan Simon lives in Seattle, Washington, and has written more than one hundred books for young readers. Her two daughters are mostly grown-up, and she misses having teenagers running in and out of the house.